Festivals of the World

USA

Gareth Stevens Publishing
MILWAUKEE

Written by
ELIZABETH BERG

Edited by
KAREN KWEK

Designed by
LOO CHUAN MING

Picture research by
SUSAN JANE MANUEL

First published in North America in 1999 by
Gareth Stevens Publishing
1555 North RiverCenter Drive, Suite 201
Milwaukee, Wisconsin 53212 USA

For a free color catalog describing Gareth
Stevens' list of high-quality books and multimedia
programs, call
1-800-542-2595 (USA)
or 1-800-461-9120 (Canada).
Gareth Stevens Publishing's Fax: (414) 225-0377.
See our catalog, too, on the World Wide Web:
http://gsinc.com

© TIMES EDITIONS PTE LTD 1999
Originated and designed by
Times Books International
an imprint of Times Editions Pte Ltd
Times Centre, 1 New Industrial Road
Singapore 536196
Printed in Singapore

Library of Congress Cataloging-in-Publication Data:
Berg, Elizabeth.
USA / by Elizabeth Berg.
p. cm.—(Festivals of the world)
Includes bibliographical references and index.
Summary: Describes how the culture of the United
States is reflected in its many holidays, including
Saint Patrick's Day, Halloween,
and Independence Day.
ISBN 0-8368-2028-2 (lib. bdg.)
1. Festivals—United States—Juvenile literature.
2. United States—Social life and customs—
Juvenile literature. [1. Holidays. 2. United States—
Social life and customs.]
I. Title. II. Series.
GT4803.A2B47   1999
394.26973—dc21   98-41782

1 2 3 4 5 6 7 8 9 03 02 01 00 99

CONTENTS

It's Festival Time . . .

The United States of America celebrates festivals from many different cultures. Americans have ancestors from countries all over the world, and the festivals of these countries have found their way into American culture. They are celebrated along with festivals and holidays that are uniquely American. Would you like to march in a Saint Patrick's Day parade? Or watch Fourth of July fireworks? Maybe you'd rather go trick-or-treating? Come on, join the party. It's festival time in the USA!

WHERE'S THE USA?

The United States of America is the third largest country in the world. It covers about half of the North American continent, stretching from the Atlantic Ocean in the east to the Pacific Ocean in the west. Its only neighbors are Canada to the north and Mexico to the south.

Who are the Americans?

Except for Native Americans, or American Indians, whose ancestors have lived on the North American continent for thousands of years, all other Americans are **immigrants** or descendants of immigrants who came to this country only within the last few hundred years. They brought their traditions to the new land from all over the world. Their different beliefs and practices have made the United States a **melting pot** of races and cultures.

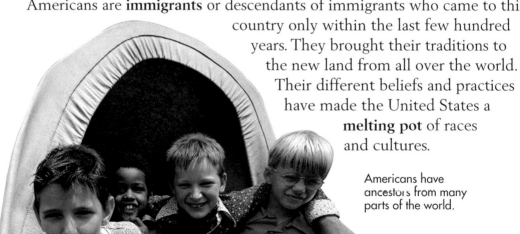

Americans have ancestors from many parts of the world.

Opposite: Extending through northwestern Arizona, the Grand Canyon is a breathtaking **gorge** cut by the Colorado River.

CANADA

WASHINGTON

OREGON

IDAHO

R O C K Y   M O U N T A I N S

MONTANA

NORTH DAKOTA

SOUTH DAKOTA

WYOMING

G R E A T   P L A I N S

NEVADA

S I E R R A   N E V A D A

San Francisco

UTAH

Colorado River

NEBRASKA

COLORADO

CALIFORNIA

Los Angeles

GRAND CANYON

KANSAS

ARIZONA

NEW MEXICO

PACIFIC OCEAN

MEXICO

OKLAHOMA

TEXAS

MINNESOTA

WISCONSIN

Lake Michigan

IOWA

Chicago

ILLINOIS

MICHIGAN

INDIANA

OHIO

MISSOURI

KENTUCKY

TENNESSEE

ARKANSAS

Mississippi River

MISSISSIPPI

LOUISIANA

New Orleans

ALABAMA

NEW HAMPSHIRE

VERMONT

MASSACHUSETTS

CONNECTICUT

NEW JERSEY

DELAWARE

MARYLAND

MAINE

NEW YORK

Boston

Plymouth

New York

Philadelphia

PENNSYLVANIA

RHODE ISLAND

WEST VIRGINIA

A P P A L A C H I A N   M T S

WASHINGTON, D.C.

VIRGINIA

NORTH CAROLINA

SOUTH CAROLINA

GEORGIA

Savannah

ATLANTIC OCEAN

N

FLORIDA

Miami

Gulf of Mexico

USA

RUSSIA

ARCTIC OCEAN

ALASKA

CANADA

Bering Sea

Gulf of Alaska

ALASKA

Kauai

Niihau

Oahu

HONOLULU

Molokai

Lanai

Kahoolawe

Maui

Hawaii

HAWAII

When's the Party ?

Halloween is a time for witches, monsters, and other creatures! Join the party on page 16!

SPRING

- ✪ **MARDI GRAS**
- ✪ **SAINT PATRICK'S DAY**
- ✪ **EASTER**
- ✪ **CINCO DE MAYO**—Mexican-Americans celebrate the Mexican victory over the French at the Battle of Puebla with dancing, music, and feasting.

SUMMER

- ✪ **PUERTO RICAN DAY**— A huge parade in New York City celebrates Puerto Rican independence from Spain.
- ✪ **JUNETEENTH**
- ✪ **INDEPENDENCE DAY**

AUTUMN

- ✪ **HALLOWEEN**
- ✪ **THANKSGIVING**

Hooray, the winter holidays are here! Help us build a snowman on page 20!

WINTER

- ✪ **HANUKKAH**
- ✪ **CHRISTMAS**
- ✪ **KWANZAA**—African-Americans celebrate this festival in December. It is a time for thinking about how to make life better for the African-American community.
- ✪ **NEW YEAR'S EVE**
- ✪ **GROUNDHOG DAY**

- ✪ **VALENTINE'S DAY**
- ✪ **PRESIDENTS' DAY**—This holiday celebrates the birthdays of George Washington, the first president of the United States, and Abraham Lincoln, who was president during the Civil War.
- ✪ **CHINESE NEW YEAR**—The biggest dragon parade in the world takes place in San Francisco's Chinatown.

What did Native Americans teach the pilgrims in the New World? Find out on page 18!

NATIVE AMERICAN CELEBRATIONS

- ✪ **POW-WOWS**—Hundreds of Native American festivals take place all year round throughout the country. Pow-wows began as religious or war ceremonies. Today, they are also occasions to celebrate Native American culture and to learn traditional songs and dances.

SPRINGTIME FUN

S pring is a time for Americans to celebrate their roots. Mardi Gras and Saint Patrick's Day are both Catholic holidays. They are also good times to celebrate Old World traditions in special American ways.

Mardi Gras

Mardi Gras is French for "Fat Tuesday," the last and most important day of the carnival season. The most famous Mardi Gras party takes place every year in New Orleans. People dress up in their wildest clothes and pour out into the streets for a party that goes on and on. At midnight on Fat Tuesday, everything falls silent. It is the beginning of **Lent**.

This man is all dressed up to party during Mardi Gras. Do you like his glittering headdress?

Below: If you're lucky, you just might catch a "throw" tossed from a passing float. Throws can be beads, candies, doubloons, or small toys.

Let the music play!

Music is a big feature of life in New Orleans. If you're there during Mardi Gras, you're sure to hear Dixieland jazz. It's the music for which New Orleans is famous. Dixieland is like marching music, **spirituals**, and Caribbean rhythms all rolled into one. Dixieland bands march in all the parades, but maybe you'd rather listen to some spicy Cajun music. The Cajuns were French immigrants from Nova Scotia, or Acadia in Canada, and were early settlers in Louisiana. Whichever music you like best, you're sure to agree that New Orleans is a very special place!

Crowds line the streets of New Orleans to watch the Mardi Gras parade.

Saint Patrick's Day

On Saint Patrick's Day, cities throughout the United States have parades, such as this one in Savannah, Georgia.

March 17th is a very special day in the United States. It is Saint Patrick's Day, the feast day of Ireland's patron saint. Centuries ago, the Celts who lived in Ireland and parts of Britain worshiped many gods. Saint Patrick went all over Ireland telling them about Jesus Christ.

There are many legends about Saint Patrick. According to one of them, he used a shamrock, a three-leaved clover with a single stem, to explain the Christian idea of the Holy Trinity, or three Persons in one God, to a nonbeliever. Another legend tells how Saint Patrick rid Ireland of snakes by driving them into the sea!

Easter

Thousands of years ago, people in northern Europe worshiped a goddess called Eostre. They believed she brought the dead winter world back to life every spring. Much later, when Christianity spread across Europe, the Eostre festival, or Easter, became a time to remember God's Son, Jesus Christ. Although Jesus was nailed to a cross and died, He rose again after three days. Christians remember His death on Good Friday and celebrate His return to life on Easter Sunday.

Every Easter Monday, hundreds of children take part in an egg-rolling race in the gardens of the White House, the home of the president and his family. More than 100,000 eggs are rolled every year!

The Easter Bunny is a favorite with children.

Eggs and other goodies

According to the ancient Europeans, the goddess Eostre owned a sacred hare that delivered gifts of painted eggs to people during spring celebrations. The eggs represented the beginning of new life. Today, this legend lives on in the Easter Bunny, a popular character that leaves gifts of colored eggs, chocolate rabbits, jellybeans, and other goodies for children to discover during egg hunts on Easter Sunday.

Think about this

Mardi Gras, Saint Patrick's Day, and Easter began as festivals in other countries. Can you think of any other celebrations that were brought to the United States from other parts of the world?

11

CELEBRATING FREEDOM

On July 4, 1776, the **American colonies** broke away from British rule. They were unhappy being governed by King George of England. They wanted to make their own decisions, and they didn't want a king. They wanted a new kind of government that would give them basic freedoms—to speak their minds, to follow their beliefs, and to pursue their dreams. Many people came to America in search of these **ideals**. Today, Independence Day, or the Fourth of July, marks American independence as a nation, as well as freedom for its people.

Opposite: Bursts of color fill the night skies in Washington, D.C., the nation's capital, on Independence Day.

Left: Marching to the beat of freedom. Many Americans dress up like eighteenth-century American colonists to take part in Independence Day parades all over the United States.

A day to remember

The Fourth of July is a time to remember the values Americans hold dear and the people who have done the country proud. Every year, bands, floats, military units, celebrities, war **veterans**, and other special groups from all over the United States take part in a huge National Independence Day Parade in Washington, D.C. Constitution Avenue, one of the main streets surrounding the Capitol Building, becomes a sea of red, white, and blue! After the parade, everyone gathers at the Capitol Building for a concert featuring the National Symphony. Then, brilliant bursts of fireworks light up the skies, as thousands of Americans party on into the night.

As floats, military bands, and other parade participants march down Constitution Avenue in Washington, D.C., more than half a million spectators join in the excitement, cheering for their nation.

Think about this
Independence Day and Juneteenth are about remembering the people, events, and values that make Americans proud. What do you like best about your country?

Another kind of freedom

Although America was founded on freedom, many people were brought from Africa to the new land as slaves. For them, freedom came in 1863, when President Abraham Lincoln issued the Emancipation Proclamation, freeing the slaves in most southern states. Unfortunately, news of this proclamation traveled slowly. Slaves in Texas didn't find out about President Lincoln's announcement until two years later, on June 19, 1865. African-Americans in Texas celebrated this day as Juneteenth. Slowly, the holiday spread, and, today, many African-Americans all over the United States celebrate Juneteenth by having fun with family and friends.

Above: This African-American family celebrates Juneteenth with a picnic in the park.

Left: The Statue of Liberty was a gift from France on the 100th anniversary of American independence. Because it is the first thing immigrants see when they arrive in New York Harbor, it has become a symbol of freedom to them. Although they might face hard times, the Statue of Liberty offers them hope.

15

AUTUMN FESTIVALS

W hen the leaves turn red or gold and start to fall, autumn has arrived. Americans celebrate two very special holidays during this season, Halloween and Thanksgiving.

All Hallows Even

Many centuries ago, the Celts living in England and Ireland celebrated Samhain, the feast of the Lord of the Dead, on October 31st and November 1st. On these nights, goblins, fairies, and spirits roamed the earth. When the Celts became Christians, they kept many of their old beliefs, but they called the festival of Samhain "All Hallows Even," or "Halloween." It became the time when Christians honor the souls of the dead.

Children peek out from a giant, plastic jack-o'-lantern.

Jack-o'-lanterns

Irish immigrants brought Halloween traditions to the United States. Today, Americans celebrate this festival with such enthusiasm they have practically made it their own. On Halloween, many houses throughout the country will have a jack-o'-lantern in a window or on the front porch. A jack-o'-lantern is a hollowed-out pumpkin with a face carved in it. A lighted candle is placed inside the jack-o'-lantern to make it twinkle.

Above: Carving a grinning jack-o'-lantern takes some strength and quite a lot of skill.

Trick or treat!

Although Halloween began as a Christian holiday, Americans aren't very religious in celebrating it. For most people, Halloween is a time to use their imaginations. All day long, people walk around dressed in strange costumes. Groups of children knock on doors and shout "Trick or treat!" Anyone who refuses to give them candy runs the risk of having a trick played on them.

Not all Halloween costumes are scary. Some children prefer to dress up as pixies, clowns, fairy princesses, or their favorite animals.

17

A New World tradition

Unlike festivals that were brought to the United States, Thanksgiving began in the New World. In 1620, a group of English **pilgrims** set sail for America in their ship, the *Mayflower*. It was a long, hard journey, but, on December 11, 1620, they arrived safely at Plymouth Rock in New England. It was winter, and, because there was not enough food to last until spring, many pilgrims died. When spring finally came, those who were left set about finding food, but the pilgrims didn't know what plants were good to eat, or how to catch fish and animals. Life in the New World was difficult.

This replica of the *Mayflower* in Plymouth, Massachusetts, is a favorite tourist attraction.

A new friend

Then the pilgrims met Squanto. Squanto was a member of the Pawtuxet, one of many tribes of American Indians. As a Native American, Squanto knew that pumpkins, corn, and beans grow well in America. So he shared seeds with the pilgrims and taught them how to plant these crops. He also showed them which wild berries were good to eat and where to catch fish. When harvest time came, the pilgrims had much to celebrate.

Squanto greets the pilgrims and offers to help them find food in America.

What's for dinner?

The pilgrims prepared a feast and invited Squanto and his friends to join them in giving thanks for the great harvest. They celebrated with a delicious meal of deer, fish, and wild turkeys and ducks stuffed with bread and cranberries. The pilgrims made cornbread as Squanto had taught them. They also prepared Indian pudding out of milk and corn. For three days, everyone feasted, played games, and ran races.

Today, Americans celebrate Thanksgiving in much the same way. They eat a big meal of turkey with bread stuffing and cranberry relish—and pumpkin pie for dessert!

A traditional Thanksgiving meal includes cornbread and roast turkey with stuffing.

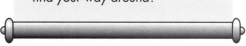

Think about this
Did you ever move to a place that was very different from your former home? Was it hard to get used to? Did anyone help you find your way around?

WINTER HOLIDAYS

T hanksgiving is over, it's getting cold outside, and snow is beginning to fall. The holiday season is coming! For most Americans, the biggest holiday of the year is Christmas. For some, it is Hanukkah. Whatever their beliefs, December is a time of joy and celebration.

Have you ever built a snowman? Did you let him wear your favorite sweater?

Away in a manger

December 25th is Christmas, a holiday celebrating the birth of Jesus Christ. Christians believe that, about two thousand years ago, Jesus, the Son of God, was born in the town of Bethlehem. According to the Bible, Jesus' parents, Mary and Joseph, traveled to Bethlehem to take part in a census, or official population count. Because there was no room for Mary and Joseph in any of the inns in Bethlehem, they found shelter in a stable, and the baby Jesus was born in a **manger**. Angels announced the Christ Child's birth to shepherds in the fields, and a brilliant star over the manger led three kings from the Orient to the Holy Child.

"Angels" sound their trumpets in front of the Christmas tree at Rockefeller Center in New York City.

Many people celebrate Christmas with nativity plays, reenacting the story of Jesus' birth.

21

O Christmas tree

Evergreens (plants that have green leaves or needles throughout the year) are an important part of Christmas. A long time ago, people believed that certain evergreens had special powers. They decorated their houses with branches of ivy and holly or a large fir tree to frighten away evil spirits. Today, ivy and holly are traditionally used in wreaths and other Christmas decorations. The traditional Christmas tree was brought to the United States by German settlers in the seventeenth century. It is the center of many family celebrations during this festive season. Family members gather to decorate its branches with tinsel, lights, and ornaments, and children eagerly wait for presents to be piled beneath it.

Family members put the finishing touches on their Christmas tree.

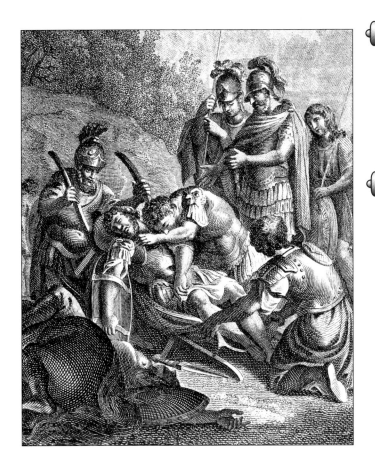

Think about this

Do your friends and neighbors celebrate all the same holidays as you do? Are there any that are different? Do you know what their holidays mean?

The Maccabees mourn the death of their fellow freedom fighter in the war against King Antiochus of Syria.

Below: The menorah holds nine candles—one for each night during Hanukkah, and an extra one to light the rest.

Light the menorah

While Christians are getting ready for Christmas, Jews are celebrating their biggest holiday of the year, Hanukkah. Hanukkah celebrates a miracle that happened long ago, when Israel was ruled by King Antiochus of Syria. Antiochus wouldn't let the Jews practice their religion. The Maccabees, who were Jewish freedom fighters, fought Antiochus and won. When they went to light the sacred lamp in the temple, however, there was only enough oil for one night. They lit the lamp anyway, and a miracle happened. The lamp burned for eight nights! To keep the memory of this miracle alive, Jews put a ***menorah*** [me-NO-ra], a candleholder with nine candles, in a window for Hanukkah. The menorah reminds them of the courage of the Maccabees.

MORE WINTER FUN

A mericans do not let the cold winter season stop them from getting together for a party. Besides Christmas and Hanukkah, New Year's Eve and Groundhog Day also provide plenty of fun.

Countdown to the New Year

"Ten! Nine! Eight! . . ." Thousands of people wait breathlessly as the last seconds of December 31st tick away. At the stroke of midnight, a ball is dropped at Times Square in New York City. Balloons and confetti, or tiny strips of colored paper, rain down on the excited crowd. People cheer, kiss, and hug each other, wishing everyone, "Happy New Year!"

One of the biggest New Year's Eve parties in the country takes place at Times Square in New York City.

Making a new start

As the old year draws to a close, everyone looks forward to a new beginning. January 1st is the perfect time to make resolutions, or decisions to become better people. Whether it is a bad habit they want to give up or a new skill they want to learn, people make lists of New Year resolutions. At the end of the year, they look back to see what they have achieved. Is there something you've always wanted to do or stop doing? Why not make it your New Year resolution?

This group of friends sees in the new year with a toast. Throughout the country, on New Year's Day, people look back at the past year and make plans for the year ahead.

Will spring come early?

Centuries ago, people thought certain small animals awoke from their winter sleep in early February to see the state of the weather. If they saw the sun, their shadows would frighten them back into their burrows, and winter would last another six weeks. Early settlers from Germany brought this belief to America.

On February 2nd, Groundhog Day, the residents of Punxsutawney, Philadelphia, gather at Gobbler's Knob, a small hill just outside of town, to watch the movements of their famous groundhog, Punxsutawney Phil. The town's Groundhog Day tradition is more than 100 years old, and residents place great faith in Phil's ability to predict the coming of spring.

William Deeley of the Punxsutawney Groundhog Club holds the town's famous groundhog, Phil.

THINGS FOR YOU TO DO

Have you ever liked someone but been afraid to say so? Are you embarrassed to tell a special person how much he or she means to you? If you are, then Valentine's Day is the holiday for you. It's your chance to tell people you love how you feel. If you don't want them to know who you are, that's all right, too.

Flowers for Saint Valentine

Saint Valentine was an Italian priest who lived long ago. According to legend, he especially loved children, and he used to give them flowers from his garden. When the Roman emperor put him in jail because he would not pray to the Roman gods, the children felt sad for their friend. To make him feel better, they threw him bouquets of flowers with love notes attached. On February 14th, people send flowers, cards, and gifts to special friends in memory of Saint Valentine.

26

Make some valentines

Valentines are usually heart-shaped or have hearts on them. Some might have pictures of flowers or little angels, called Cupids, and a short rhyme or a clever message.

It's easy to make a valentine. Use a piece of red construction paper. Draw little hearts in a line down both sides of the paper. Use a pair of scissors to carefully cut out the hearts. Then cut out pictures of flowers from magazines and glue them on the paper. Finally, write a nice rhyme or a special message for your friend. Make as many valentines as you like, with different colors and designs. When they are all done and ready to send, will you sign them, or will you let your friends guess who their secret admirer is?

Things to look for in your library

Celebrating Independence Day. Shelley Nielsen (Abdo & Daughters, 1992).
Celebration! Jane Resh Thomas (Disney Press, 1997).
The Christmas Menorahs: How a Town Fought Hate. Janice Cohn
  (Albert Whitman & Co., 1995).
Coming to America: The Story of Immigration. Betsy Maestro (Scholastic Trade, 1996).
The First Thanksgiving. Jean Craighead George (Paper Star, 1996).
How the Grinch Stole Christmas. Boris Karloff (Audio CD, 1995).
Juneteenth.com: World Wide Celebration. (www.juneteenth.com, 1997).
A Mardi Gras Dictionary. Beverly Barras Vidrine (Pelican Publishing Co., 1998).

MAKE A WREATH

W reaths are popular home decorations for many occasions, including Christmas. Why not make a wreath for your front door? You can add different ornaments to make your wreath special for any holiday occasion.

You will need:
1. Sprigs of real or artificial maple leaves (or other red leaves)
2. Glue
3. Real or artificial flowers
4. Tape
5. Small gold bows
6. An undecorated wreath
7. A large bow
8. Sprigs of ivy

1 Wind the ivy sprigs all around the undecorated wreath and tape them in place.

2 Tape some red leaves among the ivy sprigs.

3 Glue on the flowers and the gold bows.

4 Glue on the large bow, and you're ready to show off your wreath!

29

MAKE PUMPKIN PIE

A Thanksgiving meal wouldn't be complete without pumpkin pie, a simple, delicious treat you and your friends can make and enjoy!

You will need:
1. A blender
2. A measuring cup
3. Measuring spoons
4. 2 cups (450 g) mashed or canned pumpkin
5. Whipped cream
6. An oven mitt or potholder
7. ⅔ cup (150 g) brown sugar
8. 2 eggs
9. A prepared piecrust
10. ½ teaspoon ground nutmeg
11. ¼ teaspoon ground allspice
12. 1 teaspoon ground cinnamon
13. ½ teaspoon ground ginger
14. A butter knife
15. ½ cup (120 ml) milk

1 Have an adult help you preheat the oven to 350°F (180°C). Put the pumpkin in a blender with the eggs, milk, brown sugar, and spices. Blend the mixture until it is smooth.

2 Pour the pumpkin mixture into the piecrust.

3 Ask an adult to help you put the pie in the oven. Bake the pie for 40 to 45 minutes. To test if it is ready, stick a butter knife in the pie. The knife should come out clean.

4 Let the pie cool. Then top it with whipped cream, cut it into slices, and serve it to your friends!

GLOSSARY

American colonies, 12	The territories that formed the original 13 states of the United States.
gorge, 4	A deep, narrow valley with very steep sides.
ideals, 12	Standards of perfection or excellence.
immigrants, 4	People who move permanently to another country.
Lent, 8	The 40-day season of fasting before Easter.
manger, 21	A large, open box, or trough, that holds food for farm animals, such as cows and horses.
melting pot, 4	A place where different races and cultures come together and exist as a single society.
menorah, 23	A candleholder with nine candles for Hanukkah.
pilgrims, 18	A group of people who were some of the first to settle in the New World.
spirituals, 9	The religious songs of black slaves in the southern United States.
veterans, 14	People who have served in a military force during a war.

INDEX